NODDY IN TOYLAND

Noddy and the Bouncing Ball

Collins

An Imprint of HarperCollinsPublishers

NODDY

CLOCKWORK MOUSE

BIG-EARS

MARTH

TESSIE BEAR

GOBBO

MR PLOD

MASTER TUBBY BEAR

ONKEY

SLY

MR WOBBLY MAN

BUMPY DOG

It was a special day in Toyland . . .

It was Bumpy Dog's birthday and Noddy had taken his little car out to find him.

"Hello Tessie!" he called out. "Happy Birthday, Bumpy Dog!"

"I've brought you a card," Noddy told Bumpy Dog as he stopped his car.

Bumpy Dog snatched the card from Noddy and tossed it into the air.

"Oh Bumpy!" Tessie Bear laughed. "You're meant to open the birthday card, not play with it!"

After saying goodbye to Noddy, Tessie Bear took Bumpy
Dog to Market Square. She bought him a bright red ball
for a birthday present.

Bumpy loved his new ball. First Dinah Doll threw it
for him, then Tessie Bear.

"Oh, you are funny, Bumpy!" Tessie Bear laughed as
he leapt up at the ball.

"Bumpy! Be careful!" Tessie Bear cried suddenly.

The ball bounced right along the pavement and headed straight for Mr Wobbly Man. He caught it perfectly, but Bumpy Dog leapt up at him to get it back and knocked him over!

The ball kept bouncing. It bounced towards the Skittle children. But amazingly, they all remained upright because one of the Skittles caught the ball.

Then Bumpy Dog leapt up for the ball again, sending the Skittles flying after all!

The ball bounced towards the café next, where Miss Pink Cat and Mr Sparks were having a quiet drink together. Everything was knocked over as Bumpy Dog chased after the ball.

"Bumpy Dog! Do be careful!" panted Tessie Bear as she came running after him.

Mr Plod came running to the scene as well. He was panting even more heavily!

He ordered Tessie Bear to take Bumpy Dog somewhere away from the town to play with the ball.

Tessie Bear met up with Noddy again and they both
took Bumpy Dog for a walk in the wood. Tessie Bear
told Noddy about all the trouble Bumpy Dog had
caused in Market Square.

"Poor Bumpy Dog," sighed Noddy. "He was excited
because it's his birthday!"

"Anyway," Noddy added brightly, "throwing and fetching a ball is much more fun in the wood."

And he threw Bumpy Dog's ball as far as he could, high over some bushes. Bumpy Dog ran after it, yapping excitedly.

Unfortunately, Sly and Gobbo, the two wicked goblins, were walking nearby and saw the ball first.

"Grab that ball, Sly!" Gobbo chuckled. "Let's have some fun and replace it with our magic goblin ball!"

"He'll never know the difference!" Gobbo sniggered as Sly put Bumpy Dog's ball into his pocket and placed the goblin ball on the ground instead.

The two goblins crept quickly away!

Gobbo was absolutely right. Bumpy Dog did not know the difference. When he found the goblin ball, he leapt at it just as though it was his own ball.

But he was in for a surprise! Making some very strange pinging noises, the ball bounced up into a tree!

Then it made straight for Noddy, meowing like a cat as it bounced wildly along.

"Help!" cried Noddy. "That ball has gone completely mad!"

The goblins watched from behind some bushes, sniggering helplessly, as the ball did more strange things.

It bounced along making PARP! PARP! noises just like Noddy's car. Then it pretended to be a crow, squawking loudly!

By now, Noddy had realised that the ball must be magic. He and Tessie Bear decided to try and catch it.

"It's heading for the station!" cried Tessie Bear as the ball leapt over a wall, making a sound just like a racing car.

As the magic ball bounced into the station, it created even more havoc with its strange actions and noises.

"Er... that ball is making train noises!" Clockwork Mouse exclaimed. "It's hard to work out whether the real train is leaving or arriving!"

"Who threw that ball on the track?" Mr Train Driver demanded crossly as the train screeched to a halt. "It could have caused a nasty accident!"

Noddy tried to explain that the ball had jumped on to the track all by itself.

Then Noddy had a good idea for catching the ball. "May I borrow your umbrella, Miss Pink Cat?" he asked. "I can use it to pull the ball off the track!"

"Nearly got it..." Noddy said holding his breath.

   But then, making a sound just like a firework, the magic ball was off again. It bounced along the platform, scattering passengers to the left and right.

Making one strange noise after another, the ball bounced its way to Market Square.

"Oops! What a wild wobble!" Mr Wobbly Man exclaimed as the ball knocked him for six.

By now, the ball had bounced towards Dinah Doll's stall. "At last!" Noddy breathed a huge sigh of relief as the ball came to rest on the roof of the stall. "The ball is as tired as I am!"

While the ball was taking a rest, Noddy and Mr Plod
had to think of a way to stop it from suddenly bouncing
into more trouble.

"There's only one way to deal with it," Big-Ears
declared wisely. "Noddy, fetch a bucket of soapy water!"

"Ah! Good work, Noddy!" Big-Ears said when Noddy returned with a large bucket of soapy water. "Prepare to catch the ball!"

Big-Ears poked the ball with his umbrella until, with a strange "ouch," the ball bounced down to the ground.

Noddy chased after it with his bucket of water – SPLOSH!

"Well done, Noddy!" Big-Ears cried as the ball disappeared under all the soap suds.

"A perfect catch! It'll keep its bounce, it will still make noises, but it will no longer be naughty... and it will always seek out those who own it."

The ball bounced straight towards the goblins, who were hiding nearby.

"I might have known they'd be at the bottom of it!"
Mr Plod exclaimed sternly.

It was not just the magic ball that tormented Sly and
Gobbo.

Bumpy Dog leapt up at the naughty goblins. He tore
Sly's pocket and his own ball fell out.

"Bumpy, your birthday ball!" exclaimed Noddy.

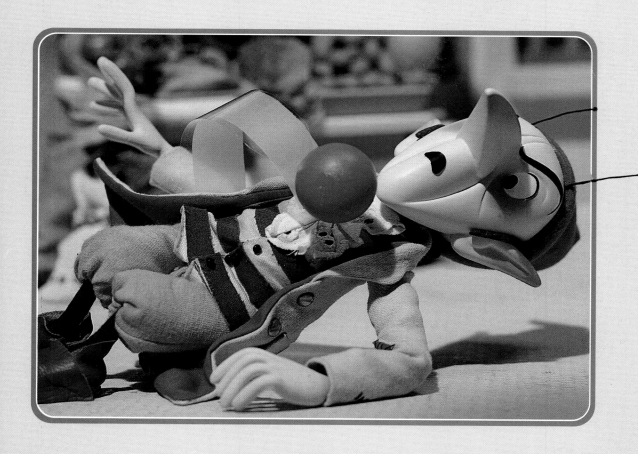

Noddy and Tessie Bear chuckled as they watched the
magic ball chase the goblins right out of Toy Town. Then
they hugged Bumpy Dog for being so clever.
"Happy Birthday, Bumpy Dog!" everyone cheered.

This edition first published in Great Britain by HarperCollins Publishers Ltd in 2000

1 3 5 7 9 10 8 6 4 2

Copyright © 1999 Enid Blyton Ltd. Enid Blyton's signature mark and the words
"NODDY" and "TOYLAND" are Registered Trade Marks of Enid Blyton Ltd.
For further information on Enid Blyton please contact www.blyton.com

ISBN: 0 00 136180 5

Reproduction by Graphic Studio S.r.l. Verona
Printed in Italy by Garzanti Verga S.r.l.

MORE NODDY BOOKS FOR YOU TO ENJOY

Noddy and the Artists

Noddy Caught in a Storm

Noddy and the Driving Lesson

Noddy is Far Too Busy

Noddy and the Goblins

Noddy and the Magic Watch

Noddy and the Noisy Drum

Noddy the Nurse

Noddy and the Singing Bush

Noddy Tells a Story

Noddy Tidies Toyland

Noddy and the Treasure Map